TIGER and TURTLE

James Rumford

A NEAL PORTER BOOK
ROARING BROOK PRESS
NEW YORK

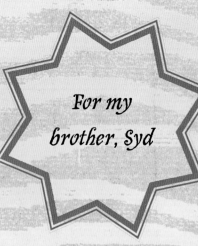

*For my
brother, Syd*

The designs in this book were inspired by those used by Indians and Pakistanis
to decorate their shawls, rugs, and jali windows. The tiger stripe design is from a Tibetan tiger rug. The background is handmade Chinese paper.

Copyright © 2010 by James Rumford

A Neal Porter Book

Published by Roaring Brook Press

Roaring Brook Press is a division of Holtzbrinck Publishing Holdings Limited Partnership

175 Fifth Avenue, New York, New York 10010

www.roaringbrookpress.com

Distributed in Canada by H. B. Fenn and Company Ltd.

Cataloging-in-Publication Data is on file at the Library of Congress

ISBN: 978-1-59643-416-5

Roaring Brook Press books are available for special promotions and premiums.
For details contact: Director of Special Markets, Holtzbrinck Publishers.

First Edition May 2010

Printed in October 2009 in China by Macmillan Production (Asia) Ltd., Kwun Tong, Kowloon, Hong Kong (Supplier Code: 10)

1 3 5 7 9 8 6 4 2

When I've finished a story, I like to imagine where it came from. I let my mind carry me off to Africa to listen to an old woman with tales to tell or to China to visit a scholar with rare and curious books or, as happened with the story you are about to hear, to Afghanistan to meet a letter-writer, hoping to earn a few coins on a winter's day.

I was walking by the post office in Old Kabul, when a letter-writer sitting on the steps caught my eye. I smiled. He bade me approach.

Adjusting his silver-rimmed glasses, he asked, "Would you like a letter written?"

"No," I said. "I can already write."

"Clever you are," he said, grinning. "Then perhaps you'd like a story, an entertaining tale that I heard many years ago in India. *Beya, seb*," he said. "Come. Sit down. I write fast."

He took from his leather bag a sheet of clean paper, chose a reed pen with a sharp tip, opened his bottle of ink, and began twining a ribbon of Persian words across the page, whisper-singing the story as he went.

When he was finished, he looked up. "Here, take this home and read it, for in it a bit of wisdom lies, I'd guess."

I carefully took the sheet of words, still wet and glistening in the January sun. *Pinjah afghani*," he said. "Fifty cents."

—James Rumford

Once upon a never time,
there lived in
the same forest
a tiger and a turtle.

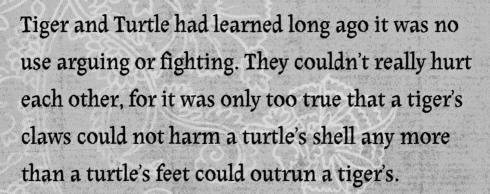

Tiger and Turtle had learned long ago it was no
use arguing or fighting. They couldn't really hurt
each other, for it was only too true that a tiger's
claws could not harm a turtle's shell any more
than a turtle's feet could outrun a tiger's.

So they stayed out of each other's way—that is,
until the tiniest of flowers floated down out
of the sky, borne aloft, we think, by a
spring breeze.

As the flower floated to the ground, Turtle and Tiger were passing each other, nodding a wordless hello. The flower first floated by Tiger, Tiger being the taller, then by Turtle, then on to the ground, where it lay.

Turtle craned her neck, opened her beaklike mouth and stuck out her leatherlike tongue to snatch up the tasty morsel, but Tiger said, "Not so fast, Turtle. Not so fast. I saw the flower first."

"I believe *I* did," said Turtle. "I believe I did, indeed. Besides, it's closer to me." And she stretched out her neck even farther.

Then, before she knew it—*whoosh!*—Tiger swiped his paw at the flower sending it aloft once again.

"Now look what you've done!"
cried Turtle. She tried to jump
after it, but managed only
an inch.

Tiger tried his best,
too, but the whoosh of
his paws was mightier than he had thought
and up, up the flower went until it was caught in
the breeze once again, and sailed even higher.

Tiger was enraged. So was Turtle. She reached out
and bit Tiger's paw. "Flower thief!" she yelled.

Smarting with pain, Tiger tried to rip Turtle
apart, but she hid inside her shell. "Try it!"
came her muffled voice.

With that, Tiger took a giant swipe at
Turtle and launched her into the air.
"Now you can be as close as you
want to your precious flower."

Up Turtle sailed, past the flower, which she
strained to grab hold of, even as she flew through
the air. On Turtle went, until, reaching the clouds,

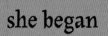

she began

falling

back down

to Earth.

Fortunately for Turtle, and for our story, she
landed right in her favorite pond. A perfect dive
it was, sending up the tiniest plume of water
as she disappeared safe and sound beneath
the surface.

Forgetting how lucky she was to be alive,
Turtle lay there at the bottom of the pond,
burbling angry words and filling her
mind with thoughts of revenge.

Tiger was angry, too, and stomped off. As it
happened, he came to the very same pond and
decided to take a swim, as Tigers love to do.
"If by some miracle," he growled, "Turtle makes
it back to Earth, I'll give her a swipe that'll send
her to the Moon!"

"Yes, the Moon," said Tiger smiling to himself as
he waded deeper and deeper into the cool water.
Turtle, meanwhile, was inching her way closer
and closer. "How refreshing!" exclaimed Tiger.

At that, Turtle chomped down on Tiger's back.

"Y E E E A O W !"

Tiger flew out of the water and began racing down
the hill, trying to shake Turtle from his back. Turtle
by now had clearly bitten off more than she could
chew. All she could do was hang on for dear life.

Even so, every time that Tiger tried to buck her off, Turtle managed to get in a nip or two, which only spurred Tiger on. Faster and faster they went, unaware of the cliff ahead.

Unable to stop,
they rocketed over the edge,
leaving the Earth
                    far,
                  far
                below.

Then, as if out of fuel,

down,

down,

down

they plummeted,

landing, happily for them
and for our story,

in a pillowy field of some rather familiar spring flowers.

"Oh!" said Turtle. "There are thousands of them."

"Oh," said Tiger. "How silly we've been!"

"Want to go back to the pond?" asked Turtle.

"Yes. Want a ride?" asked Tiger.

Turtle smiled, and Tiger did, too.
And with that, just that, Tiger and Turtle
became the best of friends.

DATE DUE

FEB 0 8 2011			
NOV 0 4 2012			
NOV 1 6 2014			
GAYLORD			PRINTED IN U.S.A.